A Captain of Industry

Upton Sinclair

Contents

A CAPTAIN OF INDUSTRY

BY

Upton Sinclair

A CAPTAIN OF INDUSTRY

I

I purpose in this chronicle to tell the story of A CIVILIZED MAN: casting aside all Dreams and Airy Imaginations, and dealing with that humble Reality which lies at our doorsteps.

II

Every proverb, every slang phrase and colloquialism, is what one might call a petrified inspiration. Once upon a time it was a living thing, a lightning flash in some man's soul; and now it glides off our tongue without our ever thinking of its meaning. So, when the event transpired which marks the beginning of my story, the newspapers one and all remarked that Robert van Rensselaer was born with a silver spoon in his mouth.

Into the particular circumstances of the event it is not necessary to go, further-more than to say that the arrival occasioned considerable discomfort, to the annoy-ance of my hero's mother, who had never experienced any discomfort before. His father, Mr. Chauncey van Rensselaer, was a respected member of our metropolitan high society, combining the major and minor desiderata of wealth and good-breed-ing, and residing in a twentieth-century palace at number four thousand eleven hundred and forty-four Fifth Avenue. At the time of the opening of our story van Rensselaer père had fled from the scene of the trouble and was passing the time playing billiards with some sympathetic friends, and when the telephone-bell rang they opened some champagne and drank to the health of van Rensselaer fils. Later on, when the father stood in the darkened apartment and gazed upon the red and purple mite of life, proud emotions swelled high in his heart, and he vowed that he would make a gentleman of Robert van Rensselaer,—a gentleman after the pattern of his father.

At the outset of the career of my hero I have to note the amount of attention which he received from the press, and from an anxious public. Mr. Chauncey van Rensselaer was wealthy, according to New York and Fifth Avenue standards, and Baby van Rensselaer was provided with an introductory outfit of costumes at an estimated cost of seventeen thousand dollars. I have a file of van Rensselaer clippings, and would quote the elaborate descriptions, and preserve them to a grateful posterity; but in the meantime Master Robert van Rensselaer would be grown up. I pass on to the time when he was a growing boy, with two governesses, and several tutors, and a groom, and such other attendants as every boy has to have.

III

MANY lads would have been spoiled by so much attention; and so it is only fair to say at the outset that "Robbie" was never spoiled; that to the end of his days he was what is known as "a good fellow," and that it was only when he could not have what he wanted that anger ever appeared in his eyes.

Before many more years he went away to a great rich school, followed by the prayers of a family, and by the valet and the groom. There he had a suite of rooms, and two horses, and a pair of dogs with pedigrees longer than his own; and there he learned to smoke a brand of choice cigarettes, and to play poker, and to take a proper interest in race-track doings. There also, just when he was ready to come away and to take a great college by storm, Robbie met with an exciting adventure. This is a work of realism, and works of realism always go into detail as to such matters; and so it must be explained that Robbie fell desperately in love with a pretty girl who lived in the country near the school; and that Robbie was young and handsome and wealthy and witty, and by no means disposed to put up with not having his own way; and that he had it; and that when he came to leave school, the girl fled from home and followed him; and that there were some blissful months in the city, and then some complications; and that when the crisis came Robbie was just on the point of getting married when the curiosity of his father was excited by his heavy financial demands; and, finally, that Mr. Chauncey van Rensselaer and Mr. Robert van Rensselaer held an interview in the former's study.

"Now, Robbie," said he, "how long has this been going on?"

"About a year, sir," said Robbie, gazing at the floor.

"A year? Humph! And why didn't you tell me about it when you first got into trouble?"

"I—I didn't like to," said Robbie.

"To be sure," said the father, "boys have no business in such scrapes; but still, when you get in them, it is your duty to tell me. And so you want to get married?"

"I—I love her," said the other, turning various shades of red as he found the words sounding queer.

"But, Robbie," protested van Rensselaer père, "one doesn't marry all the women one loves."

Then, after a little pause, the father continued gravely, "Now, my boy, tell me where she is, and I'll arrange it for you."

Robbie started. "You won't be cross to her?" he pleaded.

"Of course not," said the father. "I am never cross with any one. It will all be settled happily, I promise you."

And so a day or two later it was announced that Robbie was going abroad for a year's tour; and when he sought Daisy to bid her good-by, it was reported that Daisy had left for the West—a circumstance which caused Robbie several days' anxiety.

IV

My hero had gone abroad with a congenial friend a little older than himself, and the two stayed considerably over their time and enjoyed themselves immensely. They were plentifully provided with money, and Robbie had been told that he might do anything he liked, except get married. Therefore they wandered through all the cities of Europe, and saw all the beautiful things of the past, and all the gay things of the present. They stopped at the best hotels, and everywhere they went men bowed before them, and fled to do their bidding. Also there were many beautiful women who did their best to make Robbie happy. Robert was always a favorite with the girls, being a generous-hearted boy; he always paid for what he got, and paid the very highest prices in the market. He hired a pretty little yacht and took his friend and some congenial ladies for a beautiful trip upon the Mediterranean; and the sky was blue and the air warm, and Robbie stretched himself upon the deck, and basked in the sunlight and imbibed the soft fragrance of cigars and perfumes, and opened his heart and was happy as never in his life before.

After which the two travellers turned homeward again. There was some thought of Robbie's going to college; in fact, he hired chambers and started, at some expense. But it was only for a year, for Robbie had seen too much of the world to go back into a college chrysalis, and when it was evident that he could not get through his exams, he quit and came back to New York to stay.

V

AND now you may behold him fairly settled at the task that fate had set before him,—that of being a gentleman like his father. No suggestions were offered—he managed it all in his own way. He took a suite of rooms, and furnished them so that they were a joy to the few eyes that ever beheld them, and were described by the society journals as one of the great educational influences of the city. Also he joined some of the clubs, and took a box at the opera, and did everything else that was necessary to a young man of his station. It must be understood that Robbie moved in the highest "circles," and was invited to dinner-parties and balls where only a choice two dozen could go. He had a reputation as a golfer and polo player, and was one of Newport's most far-famed yachtsmen; but of course it was upon his automobile records that his reputation really rested. He was daily to be seen speeding about the metropolis in his favorite machine, The Green Ghost, and now and then he sent his valet to court to pay his fines. On the one unfortunate occasion when he killed a little boy, the parents of the child were made happy forever by Robbie's princely munificence.

Also Robbie was making a reputation as a clubman and bon vivant. He knew a great deal about the world by that time; in fact, he knew everything there was to know about it; he had watched men, and understood them thoroughly, and all their ways. I would not have it imagined that he was a cynic, having already stated that he was the best-hearted fellow in the world; but he had a certain dry manner which was not to be imitated, and when he told an anecdote all the world stopped to listen. Robbie's stories were on all sorts of themes; but of course telling the truth about a man does not include telling his stories, even in the most realistic of biographies.

I would not have any one get the idea that my hero was bad; on the contrary, he was a member of a church whose orthodoxy and respectability were beyond cavil, and every Sunday morning he escorted some exquisitely gowned young lady of his set to listen to the famous eloquence of the rector, the Reverend Doctor Lettuce Spray. Also whenever the church gave a fair for the benefit of the Fiji Islanders, Robbie bought up all the shares left over in the raffles, and allowed the young ladies to pin bouquets in his button-hole. In addition he actually taught Sunday-school for six whole weeks, at a time when he was desperately enamoured of a certain young lady who did likewise; bearing bravely all the chaffing on the subject, he put away Les Œuvres de T. Gautier from his table and primed up every Saturday night and taught little boys how the good Lord made the fleece of Gideon to stay dry, and caused the soldiers to fall down to drink out of the stream, and did other unusual things calculated to impress little boys. Nothing came of this Sunday-school adventure, however, for van Rensselaer père was of the opinion that the young lady was nothing like the match Robbie ought to make; and so the young man's affections returned to an elegantly furnished flat on the West Side, where there was a liberal stock of champagne and fine cigars, and two young ladies of Robbie's acquaintance. Three or four evenings every week you might have seen his automobile, and the automobiles of several friends, drawn up before the door of this apartment-house, and might have heard evidence to the fact that Robbie was happy, as so good-hearted a young fellow deserved to be.

VI

ENOUGH has been told about Mr. Robert van Rensselaer's early period to in-dicate how those pleasant days were passed. Including the suite, the flat, and the clubs, the automobile, the yacht, and the polo stud, our friend's total expenses came to something in the neighborhood of three hundred thousand a year. And since, if he had been a master-poet, or an inspired musician, or a prophet with a new mes-sage for mankind, society would have paid about one one-thousandth of that sum to keep him alive, it is apparent that he was considered by society to be equivalent to one thousand such hypothetical persons.

This idyllic existence continued for about three years all together; and then one bright winter day Robbie was invited to pay a call upon his father at his office, where the two had a long and serious conversation.

"Now, Robbie," said van Rensselaer senior, "I haven't objected to your wild oats. That's every young fellow's right, and you haven't gone beyond the limit. I have always meant to give my son everything a gentleman ought to have; but now I think it's about time you'd had enough—don't you?"

"Um-m," said Robbie, meditatively, "I hadn't thought about it."

"You know," said van Rensselaer père, "the life of man isn't all play. We have some serious duties in the world we owe something to society."

"Yes," said Robbie, "I suppose so. But it's the hell of a nuisance."

"It may seem so," said the other; "but one can get interested in the end."

"Perhaps so," admitted Robbie, dubiously.

"What I mean," said the father, "is that it's time you got ready to take your place in the world. You've seen life pretty much, and you know what I mean. You can't always be your father's son; you'll have to be yourself. I may die some day, and then somebody'll have to take over my affairs. Then, too, you might want to marry; you've wanted to twice already, you know" (Robbie blushed), "and if you have a family, you'll find they'll expect from you pretty much what you've had from me. The life of man, my boy, is a battle; and there comes a time when every one has to fight it."

Robbie had never known his father to be philosophical before, and found it a curious experience; their talk was prolonged late into the afternoon, and by that time Robbie had expressed his willingness to make an effort to perform some of his duties to society.

VII

ROBBIE'S father was president and chief stockholder of a certain vast manufacturing establishment; he was also a capitalist of national reputation, and a man whose hand was often felt by the stock markets of the world. Robbie knew about these things vaguely, and was not uncurious to know more; and so he took to rising at ten o'clock in the morning, and to turning his automobile down-townward; and his clubs saw him less and less often, and heard his merry laugh almost never.

For a strange change came over Robbie. I do not know how I can better explain the phenomenon than by his father's words already quoted—that he was learning that the life of man is a battle. Formerly all that he had known had been the play side of it. When one goes in for a game of golf, he lays out all his cleverness and skill, and gets nothing but a silver cup and some newspaper clippings for the trouble; but when he plays at stocks, he gets real prizes of hard cash and negotiable securities.

Mr. Robert van Rensselaer had set to work to learn the rules of this new game; and as he was a clever fellow, and had, besides, all the capital any one could need, it came about quickly that his name was one men reckoned with. He carried out some strokes that perplexed his adoring father, and it was not very long before the latter ceased to have to sign checks to the credit of his son's bank account. Before five years were past "young van Rensselaer" had taken his seat at the council-boards of several great corporations, and the things that he said there were always attended to; or if they were not he was apt to turn elsewhere, and in such cases it was generally not long before some one was sorry.

And of course this could not take place without producing a change in him. To be sure, he was still "Robbie" to his old friends, and still as good-hearted a fellow as ever lived; to be sure, likewise, he still kept the yacht, and the automobile, and the flat. But before this he had never had an enemy, and now he had thousands;

and every day his time was given up to a desperate hand-to-hand combat, as grim as any jungle ever saw. And so his mouth became set and his brow knit; and since he no longer had his way with absolute regularity, his temper was not so sweet as before.

It is of importance to explain this, because our friend was much in the papers in those days, and secured a great deal of notoriety through an unfortunate exhibition of ill temper. It happened at a time when he had been for over ten years the new man we have pictured, and had supplanted his father as the president of a large and important manufacturing concern. The reader will perhaps divine that I refer to the historic Hungerville Steel Mills, and to the occasion of the great Hungerville strike that once shook the country.

VIII

THE Hungerville Mills Company was one of the creations of the financial genius of van Rensselaer senior; the mills had existed before, but they had been run by several rival companies, which were always at war with each other, with the consequence that their stock was a by-word among men. But one day a rumor went flying through Wall Street, and then the stocks of those companies began to climb the ladder two steps at a time. And when they had once risen they stayed risen, and stood before the world like prosperity upon a monument. Robert van Rensselaer had quietly secured a controlling interest in them; and a few weeks later their affairs were combined, and the career of the Hungerville Mills Company began.

There was war, of course, from the very beginning, a war of rates that broke the smaller mills by the dozen. The company nearly killed itself, and came still nearer to killing its employees. It ran for months at a loss, and on money furnished by the grim, far-seeing president; until at last came the time when the rivals went to smash, and afterward prices went soaring, and the Hungerville Company was safe.

The mill employees had helped to bear these trials; and so they afterward submitted a new schedule, asking twenty per cent raise. They got five per cent, and the world seemed rosy indeed. But very soon the price of steel billets, the standard of the wages, began to go down, as fast as the prices of all other steel things rose;

and men noticed how the new tariff act made the duty on billets so very low, and wondered if the Company had known anything about it.

It was several years after all this that there came the dreadful winter when the snow lay two feet deep in the streets, and the price of coal went five per cent higher a month; and then the Hungerville Company, in the person of its new president, began to be pestered by delegations from this union and that union, a very annoying thing to the president, who was new at the business. No one must imagine, of course, that he was harsh in the matter. I might quote the experience of the good clergyman who had been persuaded by the unions to plead for them, and narrate how the president told him several capital stories, and finally begged off because he had an engagement to a poker party that night, and laughingly promised the clergyman all his winnings to help the poor along. And what could a good clergyman say to that—especially as Mr. van Rensselaer had only a few months ago donated to the same church a wonderful window representing the miracle of the loaves and fishes?

IX

THE dreadful winter passed by without change, and without the promised rise in the price of billets. The Hungerville Savings Bank suspended business, because deposits were so few; and the Hungerville constables had their hands full preventing incendiary speeches to the excited crowds that filled the Hungerville saloons. But all through the long panting summer the giant mills toiled on, turning out their tens of thousands of dollars and thousands of tons of steel every day. The delegations could no longer see the president, for the Aurora, the magnificent single-sticker built for Robert van Rensselaer at a cost of two hundred and fifty thousand dollars, was in those days electrifying the country by her wonderful performances at Newport.

And then came the chill days of autumn and the prospect of another dreadful winter, with the price of billets three per cent lower yet. Mr. Robert van Rensselaer's palatial steam yacht, the Comet, was about to start on a trip down the coast of Florida, when he was called to Hungerville by an urgent telegram, saying that the crisis was at hand.

And truly there was some bad feeling—even the president could see that; when one walked about the streets of Hungerville, he saw pale, sickly children, bent and haggard women, and men glaring at him from under lowering brows. He saw houses out of repair, and starving people being turned away from them. He saw angry crowds harangued by wild-eyed men, in Polish and other strange tongues.

These things the president noticed as his carriage whirled through the streets, but they did not daunt him, and after a long and angry conference the delegates of the unions came back to report that all concessions had been refused. The next morning men read in the papers that the unions had demanded a final conference, and that if nothing was granted, then there would be a strike, and a war to the end.

X

IN the first place, the president was in an angry mood when he went to that conference. The sailing of the Comet had had to be postponed yet another day, and besides that a stone had been flung at his head only five minutes before. I mention the stone particularly because, as I have said, an unfortunate incident occurred at the conference.

They sat at a long table one October afternoon,—eight men, seven of them pale and trembling, fingering their hats and gazing about them nervously, with long agony written on their faces, a certain hunted look that sportsmen know, but do not heed.

And Mr. Robert van Rensselaer—it has been some time since we have looked at him. He was a gentleman of forty now, grown somewhat portly and a little florid, but not too much so. He had always been a man of distinction—you would have taken him for a diplomat, or a general, at the very least.

He was a little pale just then about the lips, and he began the conference in a tone whose calmness any one could have told was forced. He began at the beginning—he explained the losses of the mills, and how they were barely established now. He mentioned the new machinery, and showed the cost of it. He laid before them a great mass of papers, and made plain how the new machinery had increased the output and been equivalent to a raise. He went on to the price of billets, he showed the state of the market with elaborately marshalled figures, and proved what the price must soon be. To all of which, a speech of nearly two hours, the men listened fixedly.

Afterward one of the delegates, a little wiry, black-bearded Hungarian, took up the question. He wandered from the point at once, discussing the price of food, and the condition of the workingmen, much to the president's annoyance. The latter tried to bring him back to the point at issue—he returned to the papers again, and they argued back and forth for a long time. Several times Mr. van Rensselaer choked down an angry word.

"You talk to me about the condition of the workingmen," he exclaimed, tapping on the table with his pencil. "But how can I help the condition of the workingmen? You say his wages are not living wages—but who can decide a question such as that? What one man can live on, another cannot. What if the workingmen spend much of their wages in intemperance, and then tell me they cannot live? What—" But then the president stopped, and frowning with annoyance, went on in a different voice: "But there is no use arguing about such questions as that! I have tried to explain to you the state of the market, and just what the Company can do. I can do nothing more. You must remember that we have trials, also, and that ruin is possible for companies, too. The laws of economy apply to companies just as well as men; there are living wages for companies—"

The president stopped, and immediately the argumentative delegate observed, "We do not see any signs that the Company is afflicted with poverty."

The president gazed at him sharply. "Hey?" he asked.

"I say," repeated the man in a louder voice, "that anybody can go through this town and see what is happening to the workingmen. I know of a child that died yesterday of hunger, but I don't read that any of the officers of the Company are suffering from want."

A flush shot over the president's face. "Do you mean to be impertinent?" he cried.

"I mean nothing of the kind," said the man, amid breathless silence. "But you have not hesitated to talk of the working-man's intemperance—"

And Mr. Robert van Rensselaer clutched the table. "Now," he cried, "this thing's gone far enough, and we'll settle it right now! You might as well quit your nonsense and understand this,—that the Hungerville Mills belong to Robert van Rensselaer, and not to a union, or to anybody else; and that they're going to be run the way Robert van Rensselaer chooses they shall be run; that they're run for his profit, that the wages they pay are the wages he chooses to pay, and that anybody who doesn't like it is welcome to go wherever else it happens to suit him! And you go out and give that as my message, and, damn it, don't you ever come up here into my office to insult me again!"

Then he stopped, purple with rage; and for half a minute the members of the union stared at him and at each other. Finally they arose and made their way from the room, leaving the president glaring at the closed door.

XI

WHEN van Rensselaer ceased pacing the room, he went to the table and wrote an order closing the mills. Then he sent two telegrams, one to the governor and one to the sheriff, telling them that violence was threatened, calling upon them to enforce the law, and declaring that all damages would fall upon the county. After that he rang for his manager.

"Mr. Grinder," he said, "I have closed the mills, and I intend to leave them in your charge. You will get three hundred private detectives, or three thousand, as may be necessary, to protect the property; and you will set to work to gather new hands, and in one week the mills will be running again. Let there be no shilly-shallying about it; I mean to put an end to this nonsense once and for all time: the mills are to be run, and run at once, if it takes all the troops in the state to do it. And that is all,—only that the members of the union are under no circumstances to be taken back except as individuals. I bid you good afternoon."

So he put on his coat and left the building to enter his carriage. A fine rain was falling, and he buttoned his coat tightly and sat gazing fixedly ahead while he was whirled down the street. Suddenly, however, the carriage stopped, and he came out of his revery and saw that the way was obstructed by a crowd.

They were opposite a dilapidated house, whose pitiful furniture had all been deposited upon the sidewalk; two half-starved, shivering children clung to an old bed that men were dragging out of the door, and a woman was crouching by the doorway, with a baby in her arms, crying hysterically above the hoarse murmurs.

Then suddenly the bystanders saw who was in the carriage. A yell went up: "It's van Rensselaer! van Rensselaer!"

Like a wave the mob surged about him. Hoots and hisses filled the air. The men shook their fists, the women shrilled abuse, and some one flung a stone. The president leaned forward to the coachman. "Drive on! "he shouted. "Drive on !"

The man hesitated, gazing at the crowd in front and back at his master. "Drive on!" yelled the latter, again.

And so the coachman lashed the horses, and forward they bounded like mad. Several of the crowd were knocked down; the rest scattered in terror; and away down the street sped the carriage, amid a rain of missiles and a din of curses.

XII

MR. ROBERT VAN RENSSELAER drove on to the depot, where stood his private car; as he sped away to the city he first took something to drink, and then sat smoking and meditating until the depot was reached. Here he heard street voices: "Extra! Extra!" and bought a paper. He stepped into his automobile, with the word "Home," and then settled back to read the news. There was the whole scene of the conference, with the embellishments of the usual kind, and the story of the strike resolutions and the beginning of rioting. There were also some savage editorials—it was a "yellow" journal. Mr. Robert van Rensselaer read them and smiled.

He arrived at his residence,—which, it should be added, was no longer a little apartment, but a palatial mansion just a few blocks above the paternal one. As he was still meditating about the strike, it was with a start that he came back to himself when the butler, who opened the door for him, remarked:—

"I beg pardon, sir. There's a lady in the parlor to see you."

Mr. van Rensselaer opened his eyes. "A lady?" he said.

"A lady, I presume, sir," said the butler.

"What's her name?"

"She didn't give any name, sir. She just said she must see you; and she would not take any refusal, sir."

"Humph!" said the other. "I'll go in."

And so in he went and gazed at the woman, who wore a heavy veil. She rose up and flung it aside, disclosing a face ghastly white, and so like a death's head that the other started back.

"Do you know me?" she asked.

"Er—no," said Mr. van Rensselaer.

"You really don't know me, Robbie?"

And then suddenly he gave a gasp, and cried, "Daisy!"

"Yes," said the other, "Daisy."

They sat for a full minute gazing at each other: she at a well-filled face and waistcoat; he at a trembling skeleton.

"Well?" said he, suddenly; "what do you want?"

"Nothing much," she replied. "I'm dying, you know, Robbie."

"What's the matter?" asked he.

"Consumption."

"Humph! It's been a long time. What have you been doing?"

"I've been living up north—in Albany. I took another name, you know, as soon as I left New York. There's a child, Robbie."

"Oh!" exclaimed the other. "Sure enough! A boy?"

"No, a girl."

"Humph! Must be—let's see—twelve years old now."

"Thirteen, Robbie. That's what I've come to see you about."

"So I guessed. Is she here—in New York?"

"No; she's up in Albany—with some kind people. I couldn't bear to bring her; but I—I—"

The woman stopped and gazed into his eyes a moment. Then she went on swiftly, stretching out her lean arms to him. "Do something for her, Robbie, won't you? That's what I want. I'm not for this world long, and I can't help her, but you can. I've led a hard life, but she hasn't an idea of it; she has the locket you gave me, but I've kept the secret from her, and she doesn't even know her father's name. I've never bothered you, Robbie; but do for her what you might have done for me."

"I imagine the old gentleman did pretty well by you, didn't he?" said the other in a matter-of-fact way.

"I'm not complaining," said she. "Only promise you'll find her and do something for her. It won't hurt you—do promise me, do."

The woman's voice quivered, and she leaned forward in the chair, steadying her shaking form. The other, always a kind-hearted man, was touched. "I will, Daisy," he said, "I will."

"You promise me?" gasped the woman.

"Yes, I promise you."

"All right," said she, starting to rise. "That's all I want. You won't have any trouble in finding her. Her name—her—"

And then suddenly she staggered. She lurched backward, grasping at the chair, and turned white, a horrible sound coming from her throat. The man leaped forward and caught her. She lay limp in his arms. He shouted for help, and when the butler came, sent him on the run for a cab.

"Take her around the corner to the hospital," he commanded.

So they bore out the gasping form; and Mr. Robert van Rensselaer went slowly and thoughtfully upstairs. "Devilish annoying," he mused. "How shall I find the girl after that?"

When the butler came back he inquired anxiously. "She was dead before we got there, sir," said the man.

XIII

THE death of "Daisy" came to seem more and more annoying the more Robert van Rensselaer thought it over. Open-handed man as he was, he would have thought nothing of sending the girl a few thousand dollars; but now all kinds of trouble might result from an attempt to do it. There were no means of identification about the body; and if he were to ask the police to find the woman's child, how long would it be then before scandal was busy? There are so many people ready to believe evil about a wealthy man; and besides, there were hundreds who had known about Daisy. To be sure, they never thought of it, at this late date; but how long would it take them to put two and two together, and to have the whole town gabbling and winking? And if he were to turn the matter over to private detectives, he would lay himself equally open to suspicion. One can never tell about such men, he mused—they might find out the story, and then anything could happen.

It was by no means pleasant to think of one's own flesh and blood suffering poverty. But then van Rensselaer reflected that people would probably take care of her; and that in any case she had never been used to wealth, and would not feel the difference; also that if he sent her money it would very probably serve but to teach her extravagance and lead her into temptation. So it would seem to be his duty to let the whole matter drop and forget it.

XIV

THESE things he was meditating while with the assistance of his valet he was donning a dress-suit; afterward he descended and entered his automobile, and in half an hour they reached the dock. It was then nearing sundown, and the rain was gone, and the river was golden. Van Rensselaer drank in the fresh sea breeze as he alighted, and moved toward the waiting Comet. Steam was pouring out from the funnels of the yacht, and the captain stood at the gang-plank.

"All ready, sir," he said.

"Every one on board?" inquired the owner.

"Half an hour ago, sir."

"Very well. Cast off."

And then, amid the shouting of orders, Mr. Robert van Rensselaer moved forward to the stern, where a dozen ladies and gentlemen were seated, wrapped warmly in coats and shawls, and enjoying the beautiful scene. They greeted him with laughter and merry welcome; they had cause to be a happy party, for in America there was no host like Robert van Rensselaer.

And his guests were worthy of him. Here was the peerless Mrs. Dyemandust, mistress of seventy-two millions, and of all society; here was Mrs. Miner-Gold, worth fifty-seven and a half in her own name; here was Victor de Vere, leader in the smart set and wittiest man in town; here was Pidgin of the great Steal Trust, and Mergem, owner of forty-two railroads. Here was Miss Paragon, the debutante, about whom the town was mad, and here was his Grace the Due de Petitebourse, the distinguished French visitor, who cried out that Miss Paragon was "ravissante— unmiracle!" It is boldness merely to name such company in a novel.

"And oh, by the way," asks Mrs. Dyemandust, suddenly, "how did you settle the strike?"

"Strike?" echoes Mr. Robert van Rensselaer (he had forgotten it completely), "there are no strikes on the Comet "

XV

AT nine o'clock that evening the guests of the yacht, being then twenty miles off Sandy Hook, sat down to dinner in the saloon. Mr. van Rensselaer's banquets were things that one did not soon forget; as also was his dining saloon.

There were two state apartments in the Comet; the one with which we have now to do was lit with a blaze of electric lights, set amid flashing crystal and silver. One of its walls was occupied by a great buffet, dazzling with the same radiance; and the other three were occupied by life-size paintings, brilliant with the rich colors that only great artists dare. The subject was the Decameron—the beautiful gardens with the elegant ladies and gentlemen clad in all the splendor of the time, and hovering above them the immortal figures that peopled their dreams, the airy pageant of a poet's fancy.

And the table ! Mr. Robert van Rensselaer was not merely an American millionnaire, he was a man of exquisite culture, a traveller and a connoisseur. Every pièce-de-service upon his table was of individual design, numbers of them the work of the celebrated Germain. The surtout-de-table was a magnificent creation in glittering silver and gold—"d' après Meissonier, XVIII siècle "At either end were golden baskets filled with Indian orchids of priceless beauty. At every place were hand-painted menus upon satin, promising a delicate and unique repast.

The wines of Mr. Robert van Rensselaer were one of the problems of metropolitan society; he got them from abroad, from an unknown estate of his own—if indeed he did not get them by means of a compact with the devil. Suffice it to say that a man or woman in New York would give up any other engagement for some of the wine of the president of the Hungerville Mills Company; and that when people asked him any questions about it, he merely smiled charmingly and said, "On ne parle pas de cela!"

After the soup he served a bottle of a wonderful Madeira, and then by way of a prelude, so to speak, a taste of a dry Sicilian; wine, for the secret of which a certain bank president was known to have offered a prize. The premier service was a Burgundy,—type c?te de Nuits,—a wine of a distinctive taste, approaching a Bordeaux; rich, full of fire, a little enveloppé, but of the greatest delicacy.

The second service, with the roast, was a champagne, not the kind that one buys for money, but the kind that haunts one's dreams. With the entremets was a Bordeaux—Saint Estephe. Then there was another champagne, and with the dessert a port, a new port of a deep, grand purple. His Grace the Due de Petitebourse raised it on high and gazed upon it long, the company listening with interest for his sentiments, for his Grace was a famous gourmet. "Magnifique !" he observed, meditatively. "C'est a'un gout savoureux—a'une grande rondeur! Corsé, mon Dieu!"

Such were the wines. There remains only to mention the little anteroom from which a hidden quartet sent ravishing strains. As to the company, one could not describe that—one could not describe even the dinner gown of Mrs. Dyemandust within the limits of a single chapter. And as for the conversation, when you bring together the élite of the earth, and warm their souls with a wine from heaven, perhaps there are authors who could write conversation for them, but I cannot.

XVI

At midnight the guests went up on deck. It was cool, but a heavenly night, the stars like diamonds, and the sea rolling gently; the yacht sped swiftly onward, throwing aside the water with a faint, lulling splash, as of a fountain. Warm wraps were brought, and the guests sat conversing and gazing out over the water; afterward some of them rose in couples and began pacing up and down the deck. Mr. Robert van Rensselaer, the host, was with Miss Paragon, the "ravis-sante"; but it was not very long before Miss Paragon felt chilly, and so the two went down into the main saloon.

A wonderful apartment was the great saloon of the Comet; but we have to do with only the Oriental corner of it, with its divans, its precious silks and draperies, and its lamp, with the faint, soft glow. Miss Paragon, a dark, languishing brunette, with long, black lashes and a seductive gaze, sank down upon the divan with a sigh. She was clad in glowing red, a soft filmy stuff of wonderful beauty; and with her snowy arms and her perfect neck and shoulders she made a picture not to be gazed upon too steadily. And Mr. Robert van Rensselaer bent toward her in soft conversation, feeding his hungry eyes; Mr. van Rensselaer, had drunk a great deal of his own precious wine.

There were those who did not see the idyllic side of this affair, who did not think of Miss Paragon as the tender, soft-hearted young person, but who believed that she knew quite well what she was doing. Certainly Robbie was not going in with his eyes shut, having argued the subject out with his father. Miss Paragon was hardly up to his standard, financially; but then Robbie argued that he was by this time wealthy enough himself to count beauty as something.

So his voice became lower and lower, and his words more and more tender; and Miss Paragon gazed upon him languishingly, until at last he ventured to take her hand. She did not resist, and the touch of it made his pulses leap, and made him eloquent. He told her how long he had watched her, and how charming he had thought her; with his arm half about her, and half sunk upon one knee, he went on to reveal what he could no longer hide—that he loved her with all his soul. And as the wonderful, the incomparable Miss Paragon, with all her ravishing beauty, whispered her reply, he pressed her to his heart in ecstasy, and kissed her upon her cheeks and lips.

When the merry company descended, van Rensselaer was pouring some wine from a decanter that stood on the centre-table. A few minutes later, when every one was gathered there, the host took Mr. de Vere, the celebrated wit, aside, and said things that made the celebrated wit first stare, and then slap his thigh; and afterward he made an irresistible speech which convulsed the company; and while the host stood blushing like a schoolboy, overwhelmed with all the applause, they opened more champagne, and drank far into the night to the health of the future

Mrs. Robert van Rensselaer. It was dawn when at last they parted, and the sky was paling over the shores of Maryland, past which the Comet was speeding on her southward way.

XVII

After that the cruise of the Comet was a sort of preliminary honeymoon; and never did a gayer, happier party sail upon the rolling deep, nor was there ever a happier bridegroom-to-be than Robbie. All day long he fed his eyes upon the radiant vision, and whispered to himself that she was his. And so they steamed down the Florida coast, and at last came to Palm Beach, and went ashore; there he found a telegram awaiting him, signed by the superintendent of the Hungerville Mills.

"MR. R. VAN RENSSELAER,

"Palm Beach, Florida.

"The trouble is over and the strike broken. Damage has been repaired, and the mills are moving as usual. Have retained chiefly non-union men. Newspapers virulent.

"Grinder."

Publishing Mr. van Rensselaer folded the telegram, and put it in his pocket, and smiled. "Damn the newspapers," he said meditatively, and sent his valet to procure some. When he got them he sat on the deck and read them while the cool sea breeze fanned his forehead.

There had been quite a time at Hungerville, so it appeared. The strikers had held meetings; the whole town had been in an uproar. Strange as it might seem, a considerable part of the press had taken the side of the men. There had been no violence, however, until strange faces began to appear in the town, and some old abandoned freight cars outside the mills were burned. Then a force of five hundred detectives were rushed into the mills, and a high fence was put up, with loopholes. On the third day the Company sent up a car load of non-union men—men who had been out of work for a year, since the closing of the mills the Hungerville Company had beaten down. Instantly the town was in an uproar, and in spite of all precautions the "scabs" were stoned and beaten. The detectives fired upon the mob, killing three men, a woman, and two children, and wounding a dozen more; arid that same night, the sheriff having appealed to the governor, the first companies of militia arrived.

Following that were three days of furious excitement; on several occasions a pitched battle all but occurred. Twice the soldiers fired on the mob, killing several, and one militiaman was stabbed in the dark. But the Company insisted upon starting the mills; and the strikers being without money, and many of them half-dead with starvation, they gave up in scores. At last reports the union had been on the point of abandoning the strike, so that its members might secure what few places were left.

Then Mr. Robert van Rensselaer read his telegram again, and smiled.

"Tell me, dearest," said Miss Paragon, "what good news have you heard?"

"That you will soon be mine," he answered her.

XVIII

The wedding came off about four months later, after Miss Paragon's Paris trousseau had safely arrived. Just how to describe such a wedding in reasonable space is a problem, for the plans of it were described in the newspapers weeks beforehand,— all the decorations and preparations, as well as the ancestry, possessions, and accomplishments of both bride and groom. The Associated Press sent out two descriptions of the wedding gown,—one technical, by an expert, and one imaginative, by a sympathetic artist. On the day before the wedding the Fifth Avenue church—the church where "Robbie" had taught Sunday-school, and had for thirty years listened to the edifying sermons of the Reverend Doctor Lettuce Spray, the church, with all its marvellous riot of flowers—was pictured with pen and pencil, and after the great event the front pages of all the New York papers were given up to telling an eager and expectant people everything about it that could be described or imagined. By that time, of course, the radical press had forgotten all its vehemence about Hungerville, and Mr. Robert van Rensselaer was again the noted financier, the prominent social light, the eminent citizen, and the inimitable raconteur: After the couple were safely married, and had spent a long honeymoon upon the Comet, and drunk the full cup of their bliss, I remember reading in the New York papers an address which our Robbie had delivered before the Young Men's Mohammedan Association of Podunk, the theme being industrial brotherhood and the community of interest between capital and labor.

XIX

And now will the reader kindly imagine that four or five years more have sped by; and that Mrs. Robert van Rensselaer is a mother of two children, and a proud and majestic social queen,—a grande dame,—wearing serenely the crown of her exalted station; and that Mr. van Rensselaer is more than ever a power in the financial circles of the country, a man able to make governors and senators by the signing of his pen. His affairs have prospered steadily, fortunes springing up at his command like fruit trees beneath the hand of a Hindoo conjurer. He has organized a great corporation of the rivals of his Company for the preventing of ruinous competition; and he has done other things that have left Wall Street equally aghast.

I should venture upon this portion of my hero's career with great trepidation, feeling dubious of my ability to conduct him safely amid the labyrinths of "the street"; but fortunately this story has been told by experts as to whose authority there can be no question, and I avail myself of the opportunity to quote from their narrative. The language of them is somewhat technical, to be sure; but every branch of human science has to have a vocabulary of its own, and the seeker of knowledge has to master it. All van Rensselaer's life in these days was Wall Street life, and it is necessary to give some idea of what manner of life that was.

In Jabbergrab, "Heroes of Finance," p. 1492, one reads as follows:—

"The way that Robert van Rensselaer defended the stock on a certain occasion is still one of the stories of the town. He was in the act of stepping off the Aurora on that immortal Tuesday—after sailing the race of his life—when a messenger handed him a telegram informing him that the bears, evidently underrating the speed of his yacht, had begun one more savage onslaught upon Kalamazoo Airship. There was plainly a conspiracy—the stock was going down by the point. Van Rensselaer immediately wired his brokers to take all the seller's options they could get, and likewise to buy the market bare of all cash stock; so that by the time his special reached New York he was the owner of pretty nearly the whole of K. A. except some he was quite sure would not appear.

"Van Rensselaer was angry, for K. A. was a pet child of his. He had been meditating all the way to the city, and when he arrived, the bear-houses received orders to turn the stock, to buy cash from the cornering party and sell back on buyer's options of a month, the object of which game was that the bears, knowing that van Rensselaer was the defender of the stock, would conclude that he was short of cash, selling for ready money and buying to keep his corner by an option. The trick worked to perfection; the cash stock was taken up by van Rensselaer's own buyers, and the bears, taking new courage, fell upon the stock, and van Rensselaer purchased options in blocks of five and ten thousand, until the bears stopped short from sheer exhaustion.

"And of course he had the money ready, and laughed gleefully while he sprung the trap. The options matured, and behold there was no K. A. on the market! The corner was the kind that one dreams of—the price went up by bounds ; it began with 110, and before the market closed men were offering 190, and all in vain. There were sixty thousand shares to be delivered to van Rensselaer, sixty thousand shares that had been sold short at no, and that now could not be covered at 190!

"They came to him and begged for mercy; and he, generously, told them that they could not have the stock at 190, but that they might compromise and gain time, at the cost of five per cent per day on the par value of the stock. They, not having yet seen through the trick he had played them, and thinking that a break must soon come, were glad to accept. They paid the interest for ten days, and then the corner was as tight as ever; and in the end they paid him 260 for the stock, and thus he made two hundred dollars a share on sixty thousand shares. It was long before the bears ever interfered again with the pet stock of Robert van Rensselaer!"

XX

ON the day of that curious "compromise," our friend and his victims had been arguing till late in the evening; and then van Rensselaer had taken a cab and driven up town. Feeling the need of fresh air and movement, he had done something un-usual with him—gotten out and strolled along upper Broadway.

It was after the dinner hour at home, and he was bending his steps toward his club; but passing a brilliantly lighted restaurant, from which strains of music poured, he yielded to a sudden impulse and went in.

It was an unusual adventure to our hero; for it was rather a flashy restaurant, with gayly dressed women in it and men smoking. He watched them awhile, and then turned to study the menu.

Famous as were his banquets, van Rensselaer himself was a man of very simple tastes, all his splendor coming from his desire to please other people. At present he ordered a cocktail, and sipped it meditatively while the waiter placed before him a plate of raw oysters, of a delicate and palatable variety. Before he ate them he or-dered the next course, some sweetbreads and a quail on toast, fresh asparagus, and artichokes prepared in a special way; the waiter listened carefully to the description of exactly how the sweetbreads were to be cooked, and exactly the kind of sauce desired with the asparagus. "And bring me a pint of Chambertin," added the guest; "the best you have."

While the waiter departed Mr. Robert van Rensselaer carefully tasted the oys-ters. The sweetbreads, when they came, proved to be correct, the wine was better than he had hoped, and so he felt quite pleased with himself. Now and then during the repast he would pause to breathe and gaze round him; he was growing rather stout, unfortunately, and at his meals he felt it. But he finished at last and smacked his lips, and leaned far back in his chair and began to light a cigar.

The cigars of Robert van Rensselaer were, like everything else that he used, of his own importation; the aroma of them was a thing ambrosial, and so our friend half closed his eyes and felt very happy indeed. With the wine stirring in his blood, and his stomach purring contentedly, what more could a civilized man desire?

There was but one thing; as Mr. van Rensselaer was gazing about the room, he suddenly espied it. His eye was arrested at a table across the way, where sat two women. One of them was a very stout woman, with yellow hair and many jewels. But the other—he had never seen anything like her before. She was a young girl—not out of her teens—and of a wonderful delicate beauty. She was plainly dressed, and pale; but her skin was like finely tinted marble, and her face—van Rensselaer could simply not take his eyes away from her face.

And then suddenly the woman saw his gaze, and smiled. He saw her nudge the girl with her foot, and the girl looked up at him; then she turned scarlet, and gazed down at her plate. Van Rensselaer's heart beat faster, and he finished his demi-tasse rather quickly and threw away his cigar. When he saw that the women were ready to leave, he beckoned to the waiter, and after glancing at his check, gave him a twenty-dollar bill and told him to keep the change. Then he took his overcoat and strolled slowly out.

The women were just in front of him, and he came up with them at the corner; they turned and strolled down a side street.

"Your friend seems a little shy," he said, laughing, as he put himself by the young girl's side, and gently took her arm.

"Just a little," replied the woman. "She has only been in New York a few days. Miss Harrison, Mr.—er—"

"Mr. Green," said the other.

"Mr. Green," repeated the woman, with a smile, "and Mrs. Lynch, myself."

So they were happily introduced. "And where are you going?" asked Mr. Green.

"We were just on our way home," said Mrs. Lynch.

They strolled on down the street; the man felt the soft arm trembling in his, but the girl said nothing, and never raised her eyes when he spoke to her. Mrs. Lynch kept up the conversation until they reached a brown stone house. The curtains were drawn, but one could see chinks of light, and as the woman opened the door sounds of merriment broke upon the ear. The door of the parlor was open, but they passed by, and into a rear room, lighted by a dim lamp; they shut the door, and then everything was quiet.

"Make yourselves at home," said Mrs. Lynch, taking off her hat and wraps. Mr. Green did likewise, and sat down upon the sofa.

The girl seated herself. She was still pale and trembling, but Mrs. Lynch did not notice it, conversing lightly with her new acquaintance. Suddenly, however, she arose, remarking, "I have something to attend to, if you'll excuse me." So, frowning down the girl's attempt to remonstrate, she disappeared, shutting the door.

XXI

THERE was a little silence, and then Mr. Green went over and sat down by the girl. "Tell me," he said, "what is the matter?" She buried her face in her hands and shuddered. "Tell me," he repeated again, in a tender voice. "Trust me, won't you?"

And suddenly she looked up at him, the tears streaming from her eyes. "Oh," she pleaded, "have mercy on me! I can't do it I can't! You don't know how miserable I am."

Robbie one is moved intuitively to call him "Robbie "again at such, a time, even though his hair is now an iron-gray Robbie was gazing at the perfect face, and thinking that he had never seen anything so wonderful in his life before. "Listen," he said very gently. "You have no reason to be afraid of me. Tell me what is the matter, tell me how you come to be in such a place as this."

The girl gazed at him with her frightened eyes; she choked back a sob. "I have only been here a few hours," she said. "And I cannot stay oh, I cannot!"

"Tell me about it," said he.

She sat kneading her hands together nervously. "I came from the country," she said. "It is the old story it will not interest you. My father was dead, and my mother dead, and then I had no money, and had to work. And then I loved a young man "

She made a sudden gesture of despair, and stopped. "Go on," said the other, tenderly.

"It was only last week that I saw him last," she said, "and now I shall never see him again. He begged me to go and. live with him that was in the beginning. He was very rich, and so his parents would not let him marry me. But I loved him, so I did not care; I only wanted to be with him. That was a year ago; and then he went away and left me he said his parents had found it out. I heard he had gone to New York, and I followed him spent all I owned to come. And of course I could not find him; and I could find nothing to do—I walked the streets all last night, and the night before. And then this was all that there was left—I was nearly dead."

The girl had flushed with excitement as she talked, and became more beautiful than ever. The other led her on; she told him all, for his was the first sympathetic voice she had heard. And Robbie talked to her as the Robbie of old had talked to women, gently, beautifully, with infinite tact, and sympathy, and grace. He was a handsome man and a brilliant man, and the girl forgot first her terror, and then her despair, and then her sorrow. No one disturbed them; they talked for an hour, for two hours, and with more and more understanding. Robbie's heart was beating faster and faster. She was not only a beautiful girl, she was a beautiful soul—a pearl in the mud, delicate and precious. And so he went on and on, pouring out his sympathy, and drawing out her whole heart. The time sped on yet faster, midnight came, and by that time Robbie had ventured to take her hand in his, and to sit down beside her on the sofa. He was trembling like a boy again, was Robbie, his whole being was on fire; and there had come a new blush to the girl's cheek, too.

"And listen to me," he was saying in a low whisper; "you do not know how you have touched my heart, how much I admire you and wish to help you. You are so beautiful,—I have never seen any one so beautiful,—and I—ah, we could go far away from all this horror, and you need never know of it, or hear of it again. I would take care of you and watch over you. You should have everything to make you happy, for I love you, oh, I cannot tell you how I love you! This is a dreadful place to say it; but what does it matter what these people think? They cannot understand, but we need not care. Ah, I wish you to be mine! I do not care how, but I will never let you suffer any harm. And oh, you must know that I will never let you leave me! "

And so he went on, swiftly, breathlessly, eloquently; and first he ventured to put his arms about her; and then to kiss her; and when he saw that she was trembling, and that tears of emotion had risen to her eyes, he clasped her to him passionately.

And so another hour fled by; and when at last there came a tap upon the door, the girl sat upon Robbie's lap with her face buried in his shoulder. "And now," said Robbie, as Mrs. Lynch entered," come and sit down, and let us settle."

XXII

AFTER that Mary Harrison—such was her name—was soon installed in a pretty little flat up in Harlem; and Robbie, a happy and guileless boy once more, was to be found there not infrequently. We must content ourselves with this brief mention of the subject, and hurry back with our hero to the tedious affairs of Wall Street.

For events moved swiftly in that part of the town; and even before the Kalamazoo Airship corner had been settled Robert van Rensselaer was busily planning the great coup of his life,—the smashing of Transatlantic and Suburban. About that desperate and historical campaign it is necessary that the reader should be told in detail.

There are men in Wall Street, gamblers pure and simple, who will bull or bear any stock out of which they think they can get anything; and again there are also legitimate manipulators. A legitimate manipulator of stocks, in the view of Robert van Rensselaer, was a man who studied the financial and economic conditions of the world, and aimed to drive prices where they ought to go. If a man could see deeply enough, and bear only unsound stocks and overproduced commodities, he might be considered as a useful servant of society—and what would be no less pleasant, the eternal laws of the universe would work with him in all his trading.

The story of the great Transatlantic and Suburban Railroad battle—the most sanguinary of all the conflicts of our hero, and one which Wall Street men will never forget while they live—the reader may find narrated in Jabbergrab, p. 1906, as follows:—

"It was the same marvellous grasp of conditions and of deep movements, men say. Van Rensselaer had been watching T. & S. for over a year, and watching the people who were engineering it. He had studied every phase of the problem and in the end he pricked a bubble that was shedding a rainbow effulgence upon mankind, and that had deceived some of the keenest financiers of the country.

"In the first place Robert van Rensselaer had distrusted the T. & S. people, knowing some inside facts about them. Then he had studied the future of the line, its management, its plans, its huge issues of stock, which men whispered must be watered even while they bought it up like mad; and then from certain secret information about conferences, of which no one was supposed to know, from certain suspicious movements in the market as well, van Rensselaer became sure that the T. & S. financiers were prepared for a great boom in the stock. He was perfectly willing,—he helped them along,—for the more they inflated it, the better could he manage what he meant to do. Only when he thought they were about exhausted, he turned to the other side; and so began the battle of the giants."

XXIII

No one knew that van Rensselaer was the man who was causing the trouble to T. & S., so our historian goes on to assure us. One of his qualities was his mastership of concealment: he had brokers all over Wall Street, and often they were bidding against each other without knowing it. Those on the outside saw merely that T. & S. had gone up in a way that beat all telling, and that then it had found a steady price and was marvellously active; those on the inside knew a little more; they knew that somebody was selling short, but who it was, there was only one man in the world that knew.

These things are complicated, and they are tedious; but they have to be understood, for they have to do with a crisis in the life of Robert van Rensselaer. For our friend was not a man who played at stocks; he never went in until he was sure he was right, and then he went in for all he was worth. Though as yet the market had not the least idea of it, he was stripped for a battle to the death with the supporters of Transatlantic and Suburban. Let the reader plunge boldly in,—and take our word for it that there is a path through the wilderness of the narrative.

It was on Tuesday that van Rensselaer had begun, taking "seller's options" of three days, which amounted to a gigantic bet that in three days, by more and more selling, he could lower the price of the stock. As a matter of fact he meant to give them no three days; he meant that T. & S. was to go down on Wednesday, the first real day of battle.

It was a situation like that in the K. A. corner, with the difference that nobody could think of cornering T. & S. Its stock was all over the country, it had been issued ten millions at a time, and what van Rensselaer and his opponents could secure was comparatively little; it was the market, the spectators of the battle, who were to award the prize of victory at the end. And as we have said, our hero had, or believed he had, the "eternal laws of nature "on his side. "It's coming down! "said van Rensselaer, grimly; "down! down!"

XXIV

THE powers that stood behind T. & S. held a meeting that Tuesday afternoon and formed a syndicate. The unknown person who was "bearing" the stock must be whipped into line without a moment's delay, they agreed; and on the morrow they arranged to buy up one hundred and fifty thousand shares of T. & S. and see if he could stand that.

Van Rensselaer was prepared to stand a good deal. On Tuesday, the market being strong, he had sold out every share of stock he owned, including even his K. A. holdings, including even all his interest in the great steel corporation he had made; and likewise he had borrowed upon his credit every dollar that he dared. All this cash was at his broker's, and on Wednesday morning when the market opened he was standing in his private office by the ticker, with his one trusted clerk at hand to telephone his orders.

The struggle opened slowly, the two giants sparring and feeling each other's strength. The syndicate brokers called loudly for T. & S., but van Rensselaer waited and watched. Some was sold, but it was not his; he was waiting to see if the price would not go up yet higher, to make his enemies bolder, and himself safer. And about eleven o'clock it did start. T. & S. had opened at 155, and trading brisk; five thousand shares had been sold, and then the price went to 155½ to 156½. Then again it went on to 158, and there it stopped. Evidently that was as high as the enemy cared to send it; and after a while van Rensselaer sent his orders, two thousand shares to five different brokers. T. & S. wavered, went to 1575/8, then rallied; sales fifteen thousand. Robert sent out again; offers were still being made, and his agents took them. In the board-room one might have seen a frantic crowd of shrieking, gesticulating men about the T. & S. post; such trading had not been seen for months something was surely "up" As yet it was not perceived that the bull movement was a defensive one, and wild rumors flew about: the Ghoul and Castoria interests were fighting for the road; Mergem was going to run it to Alaska. T. & S. had never touched such a point before surely it could not stay there. And yet it did stay there, while offer after offer was made. It was not till noon that it started down; and by that time the syndicate had bought its one hundred and fifty thousand shares, of which van Rensselaer had sold them one hundred and thirty thousand.

And now his brokers were shouting offers, and the price was settling steadily. The syndicate was again in hurried consultation; it was evident by this time that some powerful foe was against them in full force. Their peril was imminent and deadly; for the moment that the street perceived a bear attack, alarm would spread; and after that thousands would watch in wild uncertainty, and a single point might bring the panic, might fling thousands and hundreds of thousands of shares upon one side of the trembling balance. With only a few minutes' discussing, the syndicate pledged three hundred thousand more.

The market was in a frenzy; T. & S. went to 157½, and there held. The brokers of the syndicate were making the boardroom ring with their shouts; and van Rensselaer, calm and ready, sold them all they wanted, and every single time that they let up, began to bear the stock. The result was that its value swayed back and forth, now gaining and now losing a point, the trading in the meantime being furious. The meaning of it all was fast becoming plain, that some conspirators were trying to break the stock, and that those conspirators were of the giants. Robert van Rensselaer was calculated to be worth some twenty million dollars at that day; and that meant that at the present price of the stock he was in a position to buy about a million and a quarter shares. Whether his enemies could go that far he did not know; but he sat grimly and watched the ticker, while the fierce battle raged and sounds of frenzied excitement came up from the street below.

So the hours crawled by, the three long weary hours more; and one by one he hurled his blows, and one by one they came to nothing. He was not a nervous man, and he did not drum the table; but his brow darkened and he swore softly. He was staking all that he owned against the unknown power of his opponents; and if he did not break them with his last offer, he would be without a dollar in the world.

And so came the last few dreadful minutes of that ever memorable day of frenzy. There were a dozen brokers shouting his gigantic offers; there was one case where twenty thousand shares changed hands in one block. He emptied his quiver, he made the market reel and men turn white with terror; but his every order was snapped up on the instant, and T. & S. never gave an inch! And so the moment of closing came; and the dreadful day was at an end.

XXV

ROBERT VAN RENSSELAER paced his office, his hands behind his back. He had no more money, but he was not frightened; his trust was in the eternal laws of nature,—and besides, he had one or two more cards to play. He was walking up and down meditatively, talking to himself half aloud. "I think," he was saying, "that I've gotten all the best of the pickings; and so it really won't do so much harm if I let them in."

He rang for his secretary and sent five telephone messages. Four of them were to friends of his, Wall Street plungers who had generally worked and fought with him; and the fifth was to Mr. Chauncey van Rensselaer.

It was only a few minutes before the first four were in his office, breathless and wild. " Well," said van Rensselaer, "what do you think of it?"

"Never saw anything like it," cried one of them; it was Shrike, the famous wheat plunger. " Never in my life! Who do you think it is? And what'll come of it?"

"That's what I sent for you for," was van Rensselaer's reply. "Sit down."

And then he talked to them. "I know who's in this, but I'm not at liberty to tell. But I know that they're going to win out, and I'm going to jump on to-morrow morning with every cent I have and help make it a smash-up. I know who's back of the T. & S. people,—it's Smith and Shark, in particular,—and I know just what they're good for. I know T. & S. pretty well, too, and it's hanging on the very verge. It's damned inflated stuff—you know that, as well as I do ; and the street's just ready to jump on the losing side. The ring that's been making this fight is going to get most of it; but I'm going to get some, and I'm asking you in so as to make it a sure thing, We've only got to pile on to it, you know, and then suddenly let the street find out that it's us. The tumble will come in three seconds after that."

It was several hours before those four gentlemen went out of van Rensselaer's office. They talked the situation over in all its phases: the weak points about the T. & S. road, and the rumors that might be used; the impossibility of their being caught in a corner; the fact that thousands of stockholders were hoping for a rise, and trembling in uncertainty and terror at the thought of a fall; the resources of Smith and

Shark and the T. & S. financiers; their own resources, and the weight of their names. In the end the agreement was to buy all the T. & S. offered in the morning, and at the hour of eleven jump in and pound it into the dust.

XXVI

So they left, and in a few minutes more our hero was in his automobile and speeding rapidly up town. He entered his clubhouse, and went to a private room, into which shortly after there came hobbling an aged, red-nosed, and gouty old aristocrat, swearing furiously and demanding, "What in the devil did you want me here for, any-how?"

It was Mr. Chauncey van Rensselaer.

"Well," said the son, after dutifully helping him to a chair, "what do you think of it?"

"That's not answering my question," growled the other. "But Lord, Robbie, I've had a day of it! Do you know I hold five thousand of T. & S.? And I've just been crazy all day, waiting—waiting—"

"Humph!" said Robert, with a smile.

"Waiting for what?"

"Why, haven't you got any?" cried the other. "Don't you know who's in that syndicate?"

"Yes," said Robbie ; " it's the T. & S. gang, and Smith and Shark, I supposed."

"Yes," said the other, "just so; and they mean business, too, I can tell you. You'll see this stock up in the 200's to-morrow. Who do you suppose are those fools that are fighting them?"

"I don't suppose," said Robbie, "I know."

"And who are they?"

"There aren't any 'they.' "

"How do you mean?"

"I mean there's only one man."

"What! And who is it?"

"It's Robert van Rensselaer."

And the old gentleman leapt from his chair, in spite of his gout. "Good God, Robbie!" he cried. "You're mad!"

"No," said Robbie; "it's a fact."

"But you're ruined!"

"Oh, no, not quite, Governor. (Robbie always had called him Governor.) I've spent every cent I own, but not quite ruined; for I'm going to be the richest man in New York City to-morrow at about two minutes past eleven o'clock in the morning. I'm going to have every cent that the T. & S. people and Smith and Shark can beg or borrow, and the bank accounts of several hundred lambs besides, including my aged and beloved daddy! "

The aged and beloved daddy was gasping for breath. "You're lost, Robbie!" he cried. "It can't be! How can you do it without money?"

"I've just arranged a syndicate," laughed Robbie.

"But without money?"

"They don't know I've no money," said he, cheerfully. "But I'm going to get some more, just for safety, from you."

"Humph!" said Mr. Chauncey van Rensselaer, laconically.

"In the first place," said the other man, " you're going to sell those shares to-morrow morning at ten o'clock; and in the second you're going to sell short on T. & S. all you find takers for; and about eleven o'clock you're going to see the sky fall down and hit the earth."

"What's going to cause it?"

"For one thing, your being there selling short. You old Wall Street rounders are like vultures about a carcass—people will only have to see you hobbling down town, and they'll know there's a smash-up coming; and if you whisper you're selling T. & S. it'll come right then."

"There's something in that," admitted the old gentleman, after some hesitation.

"But that's not the thing I want to see you about," laughed Robbie. "The main thing is still to come. It is that you're going to make me a present right away of a couple of million dollars."

Mr. Chauncey van Rensselaer bounced slightly in his chair, and his eyes were very wide open.

"Two millions, atleast," reiterated Robbie, seeing that he was speechless. "And give it, not lend it. If I asked you to lend it, then I'd have to go into all kinds of explanations, and I couldn't ever make you see the thing as plainly as I do. All I say is that I've been a good boy and supported myself for thirteen years without ever striking my old daddy for a cent; and that now I want it and want it bad. You're going to die some day, and then you'll leave it all to me. And by that time it'll be of no use in the world to me; for if this stroke fails, it'll be too little, and if it succeeds, it won't be anything at all. And so I want you to give it to me now."

Mr. Chauncey van Rensselaer took a long, long breath; then he sat forward and drew up to the table. "Robbie," he said, "tell me about this business. Tell me all."

"First I want the two millions."

"Confound you," observed the other. "Don't you know if you want 'em, you'll get 'em? But go on now, and tell me about the thing, and don't be a fool."

And so Robbie told him; and before the end of it the elder gentleman was rubbing his hands. Afterwards he hobbled out of the room and mailed a note to his brokers, ordering them to sell his T. & S. holdings at the opening price; also he wrote instructing his bankers that Mr. Robert van Rensselaer was to draw on his credit for three million dollars.

And in the meantime Mr. Robert van Rensselaer was still pacing up and down the room, his hands behind his back, and a very pleasant look upon his mellow countenance. He was at that moment, beyond question, the happiest and the contentedest man in New York: when all of a sudden there was a knock on the door, and an attendant entered.

"A note for you, sir," he said. "It's marked 'Urgent.'"

And our friend took it; he waited until the man had gone, and then he opened it, and read this:—

"MR. ROBERT VAN RENSSELAER: "Dear Sir,—Will you kindly request our friend Mr. Green to call this evening upon a matter of the utmost possible urgency to him at the house of his old friend Mrs. Lynch?"

XXVII

IT would not profit to produce the remarks of Robert van Rensselaer upon reading the note. Possibly the reader had imagined that he was through with Mrs. Lynch; certainly, at any rate, Mr. Van Rensselaer had imagined it. But one of the disadvantages about some of the pleasant things of life is this fact that, when we wish to forget them, they are not always willing to forget us.

Who had written the letter and what was the purpose of it was a problem which our hero pondered for many hours,—hours which he spent either in pacing up and down the room, or in sitting motionless in a chair, with hands clenched and eyes fixed upon vacancy.

When finally he came to a decision, it was evidently a desperate one, for his brow was black and his eyes shone. He strode out of the room, and a moment or so later was whirling up town in a cab. Before long he got out and walked, and when the cab had disappeared, he called another, and entering that drove to the residence of Mary Harrison.

She was clad in a pink silk gown, and her Cheeks were bright with happiness; she was so altogether wonderful that Robert van Rensselaer's frown half melted, in spite of himself, as he walked into the room. The frown did not go so fast, however, that she failed to note it.

"What's the matter?" she cried.

And his frown came back again. "Mary," he said abruptly, "we've got to part."

The girl gave a start. "What do you mean?" she cried.

"I mean just what I say," he answered. "We've got to part." And then seeing the ghastly pallor that came over her, he drew her to him and went and sat down on the sofa. "Listen to me, Mary," he said more gently; "you're a good girl, and I have no fear to tell you the whole truth.

I know that you have nothing to do with it; but I've gotten into serious trouble, and there is only one way in the world to save myself."

"What do you mean, Jim?" she panted. (Jim was the name she had been taught to call him.)

"Mary," said he, "you know that I'm a married man, don't you?"

"Yes," she said, " but what—"

"And that I'm a very rich man? Well,
Mrs. Lynch has set to work to blackmail me."

The girl shrunk back. "You—what!" she panted.

"It's true," said he; "I've had to pay her several thousand dollars already."

"Good heavens!" cried the girl. "It can't be so!"

"It is," replied he. "And it means only one thing,—that we've got to part forever."

XXVIII

MARY HARRISON was reeling like a drunken person; she clutched at a chair. "Jim," she gasped, "what's to become of me?"

"You know that I'll always see that you are taken care of," he began.

"I don't—I don't mean that," she cried. "But, oh—I love you—I can't do without you! Where in Heaven's name am I to go? "and she flung herself upon him with a passionate cry. "What am I to do?" she cried, again and again. "How can I bear it?"

He strove to calm her. "Listen," he whispered, "don't take it so hard. Perhaps you may forget me—please don't act like that."

She was shuddering convulsively. "No, no ! "she cried. "It would kill me—it would ! "And then suddenly she leapt to her feet, her eyes blazing. "I'll kill that woman! "she panted. "That's what I'll do!"

The man drew her to him again, striving to calm her. "No, no, Mary," he said. "That will only make it worse for me. If you love me, you must give me up. That is the only way."

She sat there, white and trembling, moaning to herself. She smoothed the beautiful hair back from her forehead, and sat staring in front of her with a dazed expression.

"Give you up!" she whispered hoarsely. "Give you up!"

Her companion felt extremely uncomfortable; naturally, a good-hearted man does not like to make a woman suffer, especially a woman whom he still loves. He had made up his mind, however, and he meant to carry it through. He let her lean on his bosom and sob away her grief.

"And can't I ever see you—even just a little bit?" she moaned.

"No," he said firmly. "Can you not see, Mary, that there is no place in the world where I could keep you that that woman could not track me to? She has found me out and tracked me here already and she could ruin me, Mary, drive me to kill myself."

The other shuddered. "No," she said, "you must not do that. You are right, and I must make the sacrifice. I will go—I can bear it, I guess. But oh, Jim, I never really loved any one but you, and I never shall."

"I shall never forget you," said he. "And I will give you all you need, Mary,—you won't have to worry about money." But the girl scarcely heard him; she was not thinking about money.

"And where will you go?" he asked finally.

"I don't know," said she. "I have no home. Where should I go? I suppose I'll go back where I came from—back to Albany."

Robert van Rensselaer looked at her; the name Albany brought back a sudden memory to him. "Well, I declare," he said, "you did not tell me you came from Albany." He hesitated a moment and then went on, "Perhaps, maybe, you know a girl there—But I don't know her name," he added, with a slight laugh.

"Then I'm afraid I couldn't tell you," said the other, answering his smile. "But I knew very few people there. I never knew any one at all until after my mother went away some years ago."

"Went away?" asked the other. "I thought you said she died."

"She must have died, for she was very ill," said the girl. "But I don't know what became of her—she never came back."

The man was gazing at her in surprise. " Never came back?" he echoed; and then he added, "What was your mother's name?"

"Helen," said she; and he sunk back.

"Ah, it was an awful thing," went on the girl, her voice trembling. "Poor, dear mother, how hard she worked to take care of me—and how good she was! She worked herself to death, Jim, that's the truth."

"What was the matter with her?"

"She had consumption," said the girl, and she saw him start. "What's the matter?" she asked.

"Nothing," said he, "that is—it's just a queer coincidence; but what was your father's name?"

"I never knew anything about my father," said the girl. "Mother never told me; but I always suspected that he had not married her—that is—"

She stopped again, for his manner was strange; then, however, she went on. "I think he was rich," she said, "and very handsome and good. She gave me a locket with his picture that she said only he would have the key to open; she had lost the one he gave her."

And again she stopped; a ghastly, ashen pallor had come over the face of Robert van Rensselaer; he leaned close to her, his eyes, his whole face, looming large with horror. His hand shook like an autumn leaf as he stretched it out to her. "A locket! a locket!" he gasped. "My God! Have you got it?"

"Yes," cried the girl, in astonishment, and she went to the bureau. She held it to him as he ran toward her, and he took one glance at it and staggered back like a man struck to the heart with a knife. He gave one wild, horrible cry, and clutched his hands to his head, and reeled, and would have fallen.

But Mary had sprung to him in terror. "Jim! Jim!" she cried, "what is it?" She would have caught him, but he shrunk from her touch as from a wild beast "No! no!" he screamed, and crouched in the corner with eyes of dreadful fear. "No! go back!"

"But, Jim," cried the girl, "what is it? What is the matter?"

The man had sunk down on his knees, shaking convulsively. "O my God!" he was gasping, "O my God!"

Mary sprang to him again, and flung her arms about him. "Jim! Jim!" she cried hysterically, "you must tell me what it is—you must—you must! Do you know who my father was?"

"Yes," he gasped, writhing, "I know—I know!"

"And who was he? Who? Tell me!"

He choked and caught his breath again; but he could not say the words. As he felt the warmth of her breath and the pressure of her arms about him, it sent a sudden shudder through his frame, and he flung her away with a force that sent her reeling across the floor. Then he staggered to his feet, and with a moan he rushed to the door. He caught one glimpse of the girl's face, and then fled madly down the steps.

Outside his cab was waiting. He did not see it, and started away; but the driver shouted to him, and that brought him to his senses for an instant. He leaped in.

"Drive! drive!" he panted.

"Where to?" asked the man.

"Anywhere," he screamed. "Drive!"

And so they whirled away down the street, van Rensselaer crouching in a corner, writhing and twisting his hands together.

There was a thought that came over him every few seconds like a spasm and made him cry out. He could not bear it very long; he shouted to the driver to stop, and sprang out, and flung him some money. They were in a deserted portion of the park, and he turned and fled away into the darkness.

XXIX

AND meanwhile Mary was left alone in the ghastly silence of the room, crouching in the corner like a hunted animal. Her face was ashen, and her eyes distended; in her quivering hands she clutched the locket.

She was staring at it and staring at it, in terror, powerless to move. She wished to open it; but ten minutes must have gone before she rose and groped her way across the room. She found a chisel and knelt down upon the floor, and worked in frenzied fear to force it. Her hands were like a drunkard's, and she cut herself again and again; but then suddenly the cover flew off, and she pounced upon it.

One glance she took; and then it fell to the ground from her helpless grasp, and she staggered backward, with a shuddering moan, against the wall. She swayed there an instant, and then like a flash she turned and fled across the room. She fumbled for an instant in a drawer of the desk; then a pistol shot rang out, and she sunk down in a quivering heap upon the floor, her brains spattered out upon the carpet.

XXX

WALL STREET was crowded long before nine o'clock that Thursday morning with a jostling, shouting mob of men; the gallery of the exchange was packed; the curb outside was thronged. The London quotations were on every tongue, and suspense and terror on every face, in the very air. All knew that the crisis of the combat had come, that one way or other all would now soon be known.

Through this crowd Robert van Rensselaer pushed his way. Nobody heeded him, nobody knew him; his clothing was soiled and muddy, his hat broken and jammed down upon his head. His face was inflamed, his eyes blood-shot, and he reeled and groped about him as he walked. He was drunk.

He made his way up to his office, staggered in, and sunk into a chair. " Get me some whiskey," he panted to his secretary. "Hurry up!"

The latter was staring at him in amazement. "Some whiskey! "he shouted again. "Don't you hear? And shut the door, and don't let any one come in here. Quick!"

The man turned and vanished, and van Rensselaer sat in the chair, staring in front of him with his wild eyes. He had made his way down town like a man in a dream; one idea had possessed him and driven him—he muttered it to himself as he walked: "Wall Street! Wall Street! Ten o'clock!"

Now he turned suddenly and looked at the ticker, then rose and staggered to it and leaned there, swaying. He read the early reports, and then glanced at the clock. It was ten minutes to ten.

"Ah!" he panted. "Safe!"

The secretary returned, and the other seized the bottle he brought and drank from it. Then he said: "I wrote Jones and Co. yesterday to turn three millions over to my brokers. See that it's done. And tell the brokers to sell T. & S., and sell it just as fast as they can, until it's every cent gone. And then you come back here, and don't let any one into this room—not a soul, mind you, not a soul. Do you understand?"

"I understand," said the man, and went away, lost in wonder. The first thing he did was to order his own broker to cover some T. & S. of his own; the secretary had never seen van Rensselaer lose his nerve before.

And meanwhile van Rensselaer was kneading his hands and muttering, his eyes fixed upon the creeping clock, and the bottle of liquor on the table by his side. So the minutes passed by, and the hands passed the stroke of ten.

XXXI

It was worth going down into that seething crowd to see the floor of the exchange at that moment. A thousand men were swaying about one spot of it, and at the instant of ten they broke into a deafening chorus of yells.

Transatlantic and Suburban! Transatlantic and Suburban! There was no other stock thought of that day—there were many of the smaller firms that had closed their doors, not daring to do business on such a market. And those who hung over the ticker read nothing but T. & S.—1571/4-1571/2-1573/8,—and so on and on. The fluctuating of T. & S. was the swaying of two monsters that wrestled in a death embrace; and van Rensselaer, as he fed his eyes upon it, was himself a free man once more. Horror haunted him no longer; the excitement drove the fumes of the liquor from his brain, and he was drunk, but with the battle ecstasy. To him every figure meant a blow, as with a war-axe, at foes of his; he could fancy that this stroke was his father's, and that his own, and that Shrike's, and so on. He clenched his hands and muttered swiftly, as one watching a fight: "Give it to them! Down with them! Down with them!" And meanwhile the ticker raced on: T. & S. 100—1571/2; T.& S. 500—1575/8; T. & S. 3000—1573/8; T. & S. 10,000—1571/4; and so almost without a pause. Down below in the street shrieked a frantic mob; it was like looking into a huge well packed full of writhing bodies.

So half an hour crept by, and T. & S. still stood the onslaught; van Rensselaer had gotten help, but evidently so had the syndicate. It was as if Wall Street had divided into two armies, and vowed no quarter. And they fought on; the time crept along to 10.45; T. & S. was moving at last—it was 1573/4, the highest mark of the day! Van Rensselaer took another great gulp of the liquor and pounded his bell.

"Listen to me," he said swiftly to the breathless clerk. "The crisis has come—go outside as fast as you can and tell somebody that the Arkansas legislature has doubled the freight rates on the T. & S. There'll be a dozen people doing the same.

And then wait five minutes—not a second more, do you hear? and let it out that I am breaking T. & S., and that the Governor's with me, and Shrike, and the rest of them."

The man nodded and disappeared, and van Rensselaer turned once more to the ticker. There was a moment's pause, and he went to the window and stared out. Then it began again—T. & S. still holding. Van Rensselaer knew that the ticker was some minutes behind the market, and he cursed with impatience. Then he took a pencil and began figuring, as well as he could, with his trembling hands.

He had put twenty-seven million dollars into this thing; he had bought the margins of something like a million and three-quarters shares. That was more shares than were in existence, actually; but under Wall Street's systems of speculating that is a common enough state of affairs. The fact that impressed him was that every point that T. & S. went down he stood to win a million and three-quarters of dollars from the men he had been fighting. And if instead it went up, and stayed up the time limit, he owed the same sum instead. And then suddenly the ticker clicked again; it was five minutes of eleven, and T. & S. still holding,—1575/8-1573 /8-1571/2. He could bear the thing no more; he drained the bottle and sprang out of the door. In a few moments more he was on the street.

XXXII

THERE were thousands of men flying this way and that, wild-eyed and shrieking. Van Rensselaer caught a phrase here and there,—"freight rates—ruin them— the van Rensselaer—Shrike." And meanwhile he was hurrying on his way to the boardroom. He was a member and was admitted to the bedlam, to the edge of that writhing, hysterical mass of men who were crushing each other, breathless in their efforts to reach the trading-post. Van Rensselaer gazed at the figure of the stock— it was 157! He heard the same exclamations here that he had heard outside,—" freight rates—the van Rensselaers,"—and all the rest; and then suddenly he saw near him a huge ox of a man, waving a paper in one hand and bellowing in a voice that rang above the whole uproar. It was one of van Rensselaer's own brokers, the best of them; and as van Rensselaer heard him his heart stood still. The moment had come!

"I offer twenty thousand three-day sellers! T. & S. twenty thousand!—one fifty-seven! one fifty-seven! Twenty thousand three-day sellers—one fifty-six and seven-eighths! one fifty-six and three-quarters!"

And then again the roar swelled up and drowned him. Men were screaming from a hundred places: "One thousand at one fifty-six and a half! Thirty-five hundred at one fifty-six! one fifty-six! one fifty-five and a half!"

And van Rensselaer, mad, drunk, and blind with passion, shook his hands in the air and screamed in frenzy, "Down! down with them! Down! Jump on them! Pound them! Go on! go on!" He knew now that it was victory; he could feel it in the air—the panic, the wild, raging, mad tornado that uproots all things on its way. It had begun—it had begun! There were no more takers—the enemy was retreating—the rout was on! And so he yelled and laughed in delirium; and the crowd, crushed tightly about the post, went mad likewise, with terror or joy, as the case might be. There were men there who were losing a million with every point—the millions that van Rensselaer was winning. And they saw defeat and ruin glaring at them with fiery eyes. So they raged and screamed for some one to buy T. & S.—to buy it at one fifty-six! to buy it at one fifty-five! to buy it at one fifty-three! And there was no longer any one to buy it at any price.

So it was that the hurricane burst, in all its fury; it was not a panic, it was chaos and destruction let loose. The stock was "turned" at last; its supporters beaten; and the public, the great terror-stricken public, plunged in to overwhelm it. The price went no longer by fractions, no longer even by points; it went by three points, by five points, by ten points. Its speed was regulated by nothing but the time it took electricity to spread the panic through the whole country, for messages to come in bidding brokers to sell at any price. And in the meantime, of course, there stood van Rensselaer's bull-voiced agent hammering it down by five and by ten points at a bound with his twenty thousand shares to sell.

The mad frenzy had gone on until van Rensselaer could no longer bear the strain, and backed out of the crowd and sat down and laughed and sobbed like an overwrought child. It was half an hour before he could command himself again; and then T. & S. was at seventy-six, and finding takers at last! That meant that the "shorts" were "covering," buying the stock they needed, and reaping their rewards;

and so the awful panic at last was coming to an end. Van Rensselaer had estimated the true value of T. & S. at ninety, and so he sought out his brokers and bade them buy all there was to be had.

XXXIII

OUR hero made his way out of the crush, jostling past men who were crying and men who were cursing, men who were tearing their hair and men who were shaking their fists at the sky—all of them men who had lost all they owned in the world and saw ruin and starvation ahead of them. It was a fearful, a hellish scene; but van Rensselaer did not heed it, he had emotions enough of his own. They were emotions not easy to describe—emotions of a man who has made seventy or eighty dollars a share upon a million or two of shares, and who has been made the wealthiest man in New York in half an hour. Van Rensselaer the elder came hobbling into the office a few moments later and flung his arms about his son. "Robbie!" he gasped, "Robbie!" and could say no more, for he was choking. Shrike and the other three were close behind him, and the five gentlemen went beside themselves with rejoicing—now singing, now laughing, now dancing about, now falling on each other's necks.

I have said five; for van Rensselaer the younger, strange to say, joined them but halfway. Now he would sit back in the chair and laugh nervously, while his father told over the unthinkable sums he had gained, and his heart throbbed with exultation; but then a few seconds later he would be sitting staring in front of him, his quivering hands wandering aimlessly about. "Poor Robbie! "said the fond father; "it's easy to see he's done up. Here, have a drop." He was surprised to see Robbie gulp down the contents of a flask at one draught.

For now the strain was over, the dreadful pressure gone; and Robert van Rensselaer's nervousness was suddenly coming back. While the others were still at the stage where it was possible for them to embrace each other, he arose and excused himself and went out.

He went down to the street, where men were still crying aloud in their grief, and staggered away. He went on aimlessly, bending his brows and clenching his hands, and wrestling in his soul to keep before him the fact that he was the richest man in New York. But he could not do it; and then suddenly, with a wild, desperate resolve, he sprang into a cab and shouted an address.

He was at the river-side in a few minutes, and there lay the Comet. It was a wild day on the river; a gale had been raging, and the waves were high even in the bay; but Robert van Rensselaer thought nothing of that as he rushed on board and called for the captain. "Steam up!" he shouted. "Put off the instant you are able."

The captain stared at him in consternation. "To go where?" he cried.

"To put to sea," answered the other.

"But the storm! Surely—"

"Curse the storm!" the man yelled. "Put to sea, I tell you, and get me out of this town. Do you understand? Why don't you start?"

"But half the crew is away, Mr. van Rensselaer; and provisions—"

"I told you to get ready!" yelled Robbie. "Get ready! Do as I tell you, and don't argue with me. Get on board what you can, only leave this place the first instant you have steam up. Now go on !"

And he turned and staggered into the cabin. While men rushed about on the deck, and the fires burned bright below, he sat with another bottle of liquor before him; and when at last the Comet slipped away from her dock, he was sunk against the table in a drunken stupor.

XXXIV

AND he lay there, knowing nothing, while the engines throbbed and the vessel ploughed its way down the stormy bay. It was only when she plunged out into the open sea, and the giant waves smote upon her, that at least he gazed up again, brought to himself by a lurch of the vessel that flung him to the floor.

He staggered to his feet, clinging to the table. Everything was reeling about him; the yacht stood nearly upon her beam-ends as she climbed on the waves. The din of the sea was deafening, indescribable; for a moment the man knew not where he was.

Then the captain entered. "We are off, sir," he said grimly; "where do you wish to go?"

"I don't care," answered the other. "Go where you please—only let me alone."

"All right, sir," said the captain. "We shall keep on to the northeast, it is safest to face the storm. We shall be off the banks by to-morrow morning."

With those words he turned and left, shaking his head. He had heard that the owner of the Comet had made millions in Wall Street that day; but this looked as if he must have lost them.

Meanwhile van Rensselaer crouched by the table, alone with his horror.

The afternoon sped on, the sun sank, and darkness came, and with it a new fury to the storm. All the while he was either crouching in a chair and shuddering, or rolling about the cabin floor in his stupor. All through the night he knew nothing of what was going on; nothing of the seething billows that swept past them, tossing the yacht high up on their mountain crests, or crashing down upon her bow with deadly shock; nothing of the captain's vigil and fear, of the toil of the four men at the wheel who fought to hold the yacht's prow against the storm.

He heeded nothing at all until there came all at once a shock, and a grinding noise of something that tore through the vessel's heart. Then he gazed up stupidly, feeling that her motion had changed, that she was rolling from side to side, that the blows of the waves were fiercer.

Then the cabin door burst suddenly open, and the captain rushed in. "We've broke our shaft!" he panted. "The engines are wrecked!"

Van Rensselaer gazed at him out of his dull eyes. "Hey?" he asked.

"We've broke our shaft!" roared the other, above the noise of the storm.

"Well, what of that?" demanded van Rensselaer. "What do I care?"

"We are helpless!" yelled the captain, "Helpless! Don't you understand?—we are adrift—we will go on the rocks!"

Van Rensselaer stood clinging to the table, staring; he was repeating the words, half to himself, as if the meaning of them were not yet clear in his clouded brain. "Helpless! adrift! go on the rocks!" And then, suddenly seeing the wild look in the captain's eyes, he sprang at him, screaming: "We don't want to go on the rocks! No; you are mad! Do something! Stop her!"

The other saw that he was drunk; but fear was sobering van Rensselaer fast, as excitement had done once before. "Where are we? "he cried. "Where are we?"

An awful blow shook the vessel; she reeled and staggered, and the two waited in fright; then, as she righted herself, the captain answered: "We are off the coast of Maine—about fifty miles off. But we are drifting; and we can do nothing at all. If help does not come, we are lost."

"Help must come !" screamed van Rensselaer. He understood clearly at last. "You are crazy! It cannot be!"

And he started toward the companionway, the captain at his side. As he tried to open the door, however, he stooped, appalled at the wildness of the night. It was black outside; but the wind was a fierce living thing that smote him in the face, and the hissing spray stung like hail. Van Rensselaer stared out only long enough to see a rocket start out from the deck and cleave its way into the sky, and then he reeled back into the cabin.

The man was now aware of his situation, and every emotion was gone but terror. He staggered about, flung this way and that with the tossing of the yacht, raising his clenched hands in the air, and screaming in frantic fear: "My God, my God! It can't be! It's a lie! Save us! What shall we do?"—and so on, until the captain turned in sheer disgust and went back to the deck and his duty.

But that van Rensselaer did not even know—he raced on back and forth, crazed and raving. All was dead in him now but the wild beast—if, indeed, there had ever been anything else alive in him. He wanted to live—he wanted to get on the land— he was worth a hundred million dollars—he—he! and was he to be drowned like a prisoned rat in a cage? His cries rang above all the storm; he called on God—he wept—he prayed—he cursed; and all the while the mad storm roared on, howling outside like some savage beast that was fighting to get at him, and driving the little vessel on before it to its doom. There was no one to hear him, the prisoned rat in the cage, though he foamed at the mouth in his frenzy.

XXXV

So an hour or two went by; up above the dawn broke and the daylight came. Van Rensselaer was still howling, though so weak that he could scarcely stagger, when the cabin door was flung wide again, and the captain, white, and with set lips, came in. "It is all over, sir," he said. "We are lost."

The owner's eyes were glaring like a maniac's. "What do you mean?" he shrieked.

"Come up and see," was the reply, and van Rensselaer rushed blindly to the deck. Clinging to the companionway door, he stared about him, dazed at first, and realizing nothing but his own horror. A mad chaos was about him; the yacht was like a bubble tossed about by the gigantic seas; the waves were like mountains around her. Down into a great valley she sank, down—.down—plunging,. and van Rensselaer gasped in fear; and then a great rolling mountain came sweeping down over her, and up she rose—higher and higher—to the very crest, and sped along with the speed of an express train, the mad waters seething and hissing and roaring and thundering around her.

From the mountain top van Rensselaer gazed about him—and his cries died in his throat. Not half a mile away, right upon them, as it looked, was the shore—the wild, lonely, horrible shore—the shore with the jagged rocks and the merciless iron cliffs—and destruction, imminent and inevitable!

The sight took the last atom of the soul out of van Rensselaer. He whimpered, he wailed, he would have fallen down upon the deck and grovelled but that instinct made him cling to his support. To stand there alive and safe, and be swept thus to death, foot by foot! To be helpless in the grip of these grim, relentless forces; it was too much, it was too much! It made him hysterical; it turned him into a beast, into a fool. He screamed, he laughed, he sobbed; but the words he spoke no longer had meaning.

His eyes were fixed upon the black rocks before them; as they came nearer he heard the sounds made by the mountains of water hurled against them,—a sound far-reaching, all-pervading, elemental, cosmic. Only once he turned elsewhere, to see the crew flinging out their anchors in a last vain hope; to see the yacht whirl round as they caught, to see the waves lift her up, and sweep her on, and snap the cables like so many threads.

Then again he perceived that the crew was trying to get out one of the boats; and he bounded to the spot, and waited. He did not help, he clung to the davits. But the instant the boat touched the water, he struck one of the men out of the way and leaped in. Several followed, and there was cry, "Enough!" and they pushed off, and were whirled away from the yacht. An instant later a breaking wave struck them a glancing blow, and over they went.

Van Rensselaer came to the surface, strangling and gasping, still in his frenzy of fear. The boat was near, and he struck out and caught it. There was another man close to him, a sailor, stretching out his hands to him; as the waves tossed them about he touched van Rensselaer's foot and gripped it. The other kicked at him madly, in frantic rage—kicked him off, and kicked him down. So he clung alone to the storm-tossed lifeboat.

It was a fearful struggle: the waves choked him, stunned him, half drowned him; but he hung like mad, and fought to keep his head above the water, while the sea was sweeping him nearer and nearer to the iron shore. He was staring at it wildly, a monstrous enemy with open mouth, and huge jagged teeth that gaped at him. They were looming high above him now; the roaring of the breakers swelled in his ears, in his soul, dazing him, appalling him, poor shivering mite of life that he was. And then suddenly he felt himself sinking—downward, deep down in a valley; he felt himself tossed and rocked, swaying as if in a tree-top ; and then upwards he started—higher—higher—right to the boiling crest, the hovering, poising crest. He screamed, he writhed, it was like some hideous nightmare, terrifying to the soul. But the wave seized him—he felt it seize him; and it started—slowly—then faster, then faster yet—with the speed of a cannon ball—and hurled him, smote him, upon the jagged rocks. It battered his face, it broke his limbs, it crushed his skull like an eggshell; and so the last spark of his hungry life went out of him.

XXXVI

I SHARE in Ruskin's distrust of the "pathetic fallacy"; and I have no intention of implying that the waves had any sentiments whatever in connection with Robert van Rensselaer. It was purely an accident that they kept him in their grasp, and beat him against the cliff all day; that one by one they rushed up to seize him, and spent all their force in hurling him, in pounding him, until he had lost all semblance of a man; it was not until night, and when the wind died out, that they washed him on down the shore, and sought out a little cove and bore him to the sandy edge.

It was a still spot; there was no voice but the waves' voice, and all night long they called to each other on the beach, and tossed the body back and forth in the silver moonlight. When the morning broke it was swollen and purple, and it lay half hidden in the sand.

The sun came up and still it was there, unheeded save by innumerable small creatures that walked awkwardly, bearing long weapons in the air. One of them soon climbed upon the face and fastened its claws in the lips; and others came quickly, for it was choice prey. Was it not true that for twoscore years and more the earth had been searched for things rare and precious enough to help make up the body of Robert van Rensselaer? Think of the hogsheads of rare wines that had been poured into it! Of the boxes of priceless cigars that had flavored it! Of the terrapin, and the venison, and the ducks—the strangely spiced sauces—the infinity of sweetmeats—the pink satin menus, full of elegant French names! Had not thousands of men labored daily to fetch and prepare these things, to serve them upon crystal and silver before that precious body—and to clothe it and to house it, and to smooth all its paths through the world? And now it lay at last upon the sand, to be devoured by a swarm of hungry crabs!

So another day came, and in the afternoon two fishing boats rowed by, and one of the fishermen espied the body. He landed with his companion, shouting to the other boat that there must have been a wreck, and to go on up the shore and look for it.

Then he went toward the body, or what there was of it. The clothing was still intact, and so he searched in the pockets, pulling out first of all a marvellous gold watch that had cost eighteen hundred dollars in Geneva. That interested him, of course, and he went on in haste, and found a wallet, with plenty of money, and with some cards in it. They were blurred, but one could still make out the name on them, and the fisherman gave a cry, "Good God! this says Robert van Rensselaer!"

"Who's Robert van Rensselaer?" demanded the other, wonderingly.

Doctor Lettuce Spray preached the most eloquent of all his sermons upon the text, "Blessed are the millionnaires, for they have inherited the earth, and you can't get it away from them."

The Codes Of Hammurabi And Moses
W. W. Davies

QTY

The discovery of the Hammurabi Code is one of the greatest achievements of archaeology, and is of paramount interest, not only to the student of the Bible, but also to all those interested in ancient history...

Religion   **ISBN: *1-59462-338-4***   **Pages:132**

MSRP $12.95

The Theory of Moral Sentiments
Adam Smith

QTY

This work from 1749. contains original theories of conscience amd moral judgment and it is the foundation for systemof morals.

Philosophy **ISBN: *1-59462-777-0***   **Pages:536**

MSRP $19.95

Jessica's First Prayer
Hesba Stretton

QTY

In a screened and secluded corner of one of the many railway-bridges which span the streets of London there could be seen a few years ago, from five o'clock every morning until half past eight, a tidily set-out coffee-stall, consisting of a trestle and board, upon which stood two large tin cans, with a small fire of charcoal burning under each so as to keep the coffee boiling during the early hours of the morning when the work-people were thronging into the city on their way to their daily toil...

Pages:84

Childrens   **ISBN: *1-59462-373-2***   *MSRP $9.95*

My Life and Work
Henry Ford

QTY

Henry Ford revolutionized the world with his implementation of mass production for the Model T automobile. Gain valuable business insight into his life and work with his own auto-biography... "We have only started on our development of our country we have not as yet, with all our talk of wonderful progress, done more than scratch the surface. The progress has been wonderful enough but..."

Pages:300

Biographies/   **ISBN: *1-59462-198-5***   *MSRP $21.95* www.bookjungle.com *email: sales@bookjungle.com fax: 630-214-0564 mail: Book Jungle PO Box 2226 Champaign, IL 61825*

The Art of Cross-Examination
Francis Wellman

QTY

I presume it is the experience of every author, after his first book is published upon an important subject, to be almost overwhelmed with a wealth of ideas and illustrations which could readily have been included in his book, and which to his own mind, at least, seem to make a second edition inevitable. Such certainly was the case with me; and when the first edition had reached its sixth impression in five months, I rejoiced to learn that it seemed to my publishers that the book had met with a sufficiently favorable reception to justify a second and considerably enlarged edition. ..

Pages:412

Reference   **ISBN:** *1-59462-647-2*   *MSRP $19.95*

On the Duty of Civil Disobedience
Henry David Thoreau

QTY

Thoreau wrote his famous essay, On the Duty of Civil Disobedience, as a protest against an unjust but popular war and the immoral but popular institution of slave-owning. He did more than write—he declined to pay his taxes, and was hauled off to gaol in consequence. Who can say how much this refusal of his hastened the end of the war and of slavery ?

Law   **ISBN:** *1-59462-747-9*

Pages:48
MSRP $7.45

Dream Psychology Psychoanalysis for Beginners
Sigmund Freud

QTY

Sigmund Freud, born Sigismund Schlomo Freud (May 6, 1856 - September 23, 1939), was a Jewish-Austrian neurologist and psychiatrist who co-founded the psychoanalytic school of psychology. Freud is best known for his theories of the unconscious mind, especially involving the mechanism of repression; his redefinition of sexual desire as mobile and directed towards a wide variety of objects; and his therapeutic techniques, especially his understanding of transference in the therapeutic relationship and the presumed value of dreams as sources of insight into unconscious desires.

Pages:196

Psychology   **ISBN:** *1-59462-905-6*   *MSRP $15.45*

The Miracle of Right Thought
Orison Swett Marden

QTY

Believe with all of your heart that you will do what you were made to do. When the mind has once formed the habit of holding cheerful, happy, prosperous pictures, it will not be easy to form the opposite habit. It does not matter how improbable or how far away this realization may see, or how dark the prospects may be, if we visualize them as best we can, as vividly as possible, hold tenaciously to them and vigorously struggle to attain them, they will gradually become actualized, realized in the life. But a desire, a longing without endeavor, a yearning abandoned or held indifferently will vanish without realization.

Pages:360

Self Help   **ISBN:** *1-59462-644-8*   *MSRP $25.45*

www.**bookjungle**.com *email: sales@bookjungle.com fax: 630-214-0564 mail: Book Jungle PO Box 2226 Champaign, IL 61825*

QTY

The Rosicrucian Cosmo-Conception Mystic Christianity *by Max Heindel*   ISBN: *1-59462-188-8*   **$38.95**
The Rosicrucian Cosmo-conception is not dogmatic, neither does it appeal to any other authority than the reason of the student. It is: not controversial, but is: sent forth in the, hope that it may help to clear...   New Age/Religion Pages 646

Abandonment To Divine Providence *by Jean-Pierre de Caussade*   ISBN: *1-59462-228-0*   **$25.95**
"The Rev. Jean Pierre de Caussade was one of the most remarkable spiritual writers of the Society of Jesus in France in the 18th Century. His death took place at Toulouse in 1751. His works have gone through many editions and have been republished...   Inspirational/Religion Pages 400

Mental Chemistry *by Charles Haanel*   ISBN: *1-59462-192-6*   **$23.95**
Mental Chemistry allows the change of material conditions by combining and appropriately utilizing the power of the mind. Much like applied chemistry creates something new and unique out of careful combinations of chemicals the mastery of mental chemistry...   New Age Pages 354

The Letters of Robert Browning and Elizabeth Barret Barrett 1845-1846 vol II   ISBN: *1-59462-193-4*   **$35.95**
by Robert Browning and Elizabeth Barrett   Biographies Pages 596

Gleanings In Genesis (volume I) *by Arthur W. Pink*   ISBN: *1-59462-130-6*   **$27.45**
Appropriately has Genesis been termed "the seed plot of the Bible" for in it we have, in germ form, almost all of the great doctrines which are afterwards fully developed in the books of Scripture which follow...   Religion/Inspirational Pages 420

The Master Key *by L. W. de Laurence*   ISBN: *1-59462-001-6*   **$30.95**
In no branch of human knowledge has there been a more lively increase of the spirit of research during the past few years than in the study of Psychology, Concentration and Mental Discipline. The requests for authentic lessons in Thought Control, Mental Discipline and...   New Age/Business Pages 422

The Lesser Key Of Solomon Goetia *by L. W. de Laurence*   ISBN: *1-59462-092-X*   **$9.95**
This translation of the first book of the "Lernegton" which is now for the first time made accessible to students of Talismanic Magic was done, after careful collation and edition, from numerous Ancient Manuscripts in Hebrew, Latin, and French...   New Age/Occult Pages 92

Rubaiyat Of Omar Khayyam *by Edward Fitzgerald*   ISBN:*1-59462-332-5*   **$13.95**
Edward Fitzgerald, whom the world has already learned, in spite of his own efforts to remain within the shadow of anonymity, to look upon as one of the rarest poets of the century, was born at Bredfield, in Suffolk, on the 31st of March, 1809. He was the third son of John Purcell...   Music Pages 172

Ancient Law *by Henry Maine*   ISBN: *1-59462-128-4*   **$29.95**
The chief object of the following pages is to indicate some of the earliest ideas of mankind, as they are reflected in Ancient Law, and to point out the relation of those ideas to modern thought.   Religion/History Pages 452

Far-Away Stories *by William J. Locke*   ISBN: *1-59462-129-2*   **$19.45**
"Good wine needs no bush, but a collection of mixed vintages does. And this book is just such a collection. Some of the stories I do not want to remain buried for ever in the museum files of dead magazine-numbers an author's not unpardonable vanity..."   Fiction Pages 272

Life of David Crockett *by David Crockett*   ISBN: *1-59462-250-7*   **$27.45**
"Colonel David Crockett was one of the most remarkable men of the times in which he lived. Born in humble life, but gifted with a strong will, an indomitable courage, and unremitting perseverance...   Biographies/New Age Pages 424

Lip-Reading *by Edward Nitchie*   ISBN: *1-59462-206-X*   **$25.95**
Edward B. Nitchie, founder of the New York School for the Hard of Hearing, now the Nitchie School of Lip-Reading, Inc, wrote "LIP-READING Principles and Practice". The development and perfecting of this meritorious work on lip-reading was an undertaking...   How-to Pages 400

A Handbook of Suggestive Therapeutics, Applied Hypnotism, Psychic Science   ISBN: *1-59462-214-0*   **$24.95**
by Henry Munro   Health/New Age/Health/Self-help Pages 376

A Doll's House: and Two Other Plays *by Henrik Ibsen*   ISBN: *1-59462-112-8*   **$19.95**
Henrik Ibsen created this classic when in revolutionary 1848 Rome. Introducing some striking concepts in playwriting for the realist genre, this play has been studied the world over.   Fiction/Classics/Plays 308

The Light of Asia *by sir Edwin Arnold*   ISBN: *1-59462-204-3*   **$13.95**
In this poetic masterpiece, Edwin Arnold describes the life and teachings of Buddha. The man who was to become known as Buddha to the world was born as Prince Gautama of India but he rejected the worldly riches and abandoned the reigns of power when...   Religion/History/Biographies Pages 170

The Complete Works of Guy de Maupassant *by Guy de Maupassant*   ISBN: *1-59462-157-8*   **$16.95**
"For days and days, nights and nights, I had dreamed of that first kiss which was to consecrate our engagement, and I knew not on what spot I should put my lips..."   Fiction/Classics Pages 240

The Art of Cross-Examination *by Francis L. Wellman*   ISBN: *1-59462-309-0*   **$26.95**
Written by a renowned trial lawyer, Wellman imparts his experience and uses case studies to explain how to use psychology to extract desired information through questioning.   How-to/Science/Reference Pages 408

Answered or Unanswered? *by Louisa Vaughan*   ISBN: *1-59462-248-5*   **$10.95**
Miracles of Faith in China   Religion Pages 112

The Edinburgh Lectures on Mental Science (1909) *by Thomas*   ISBN: *1-59462-008-3*   **$11.95**
This book contains the substance of a course of lectures recently given by the writer in the Queen Street Hail, Edinburgh. Its purpose is to indicate the Natural Principles governing the relation between Mental Action and Material Conditions...   New Age/Psychology Pages 148

Ayesha *by H. Rider Haggard*   ISBN: *1-59462-301-5*   **$24.95**
Verily and indeed it is the unexpected that happens! Probably if there was one person upon the earth from whom the Editor of this, and of a certain previous history, did not expect to hear again...   Classics Pages 380

Ayala's Angel *by Anthony Trollope*   ISBN: *1-59462-352-X*   **$29.95**
The two girls were both pretty, but Lucy who was twenty-one who supposed to be simple and comparatively unattractive, whereas Ayala was credited, as her Bombwhat romantic name might show, with poetic charm and a taste for romance. Ayala when her father died was nineteen...   Fiction Pages 484

The American Commonwealth *by James Bryce*   ISBN: *1-59462-286-8*   **$34.45**
An interpretation of American democratic political theory. It examines political mechanics and society from the perspective of Scotsman James Bryce   Politics Pages 572

Stories of the Pilgrims *by Margaret P. Pumphrey*   ISBN: *1-59462-116-0*   **$17.95**
This book explores pilgrims religious oppression in England as well as their escape to Holland and eventual crossing to America on the Mayflower, and their early days in New England...   History Pages 268

QTY

The Fasting Cure *by Sinclair Upton*　　　　　　　　　　　　　ISBN: *1-59462-222-1*　**$13.95**

In the Cosmopolitan Magazine for May, 1910, and in the Contemporary Review (London) for April, 1910, I published an article dealing with my experiences in fasting. I have written a great many magazine articles, but never one which attracted so much attention... New Age/Self Help/Health Pages 164

Hebrew Astrology *by Sepharial*　　　　　　　　　　　　　　ISBN: *1-59462-308-2*　**$13.45**

In these days of advanced thinking it is a matter of common observation that we have left many of the old landmarks behind and that we are now pressing forward to greater heights and to a wider horizon than that which represented the mind-content of our progenitors...　　Astrology Pages 144

Thought Vibration or The Law of Attraction in the Thought World　　ISBN: *1-59462-127-6*　**$12.95**

by William Walker Atkinson　　　　　　　　　　　　　　　　　　Psychology/Religion Pages 144

Optimism *by Helen Keller*　　　　　　　　　　　　　　　　ISBN: *1-59462-108-X*　**$15.95**

Helen Keller was blind, deaf, and mute since 19 months old, yet famously learned how to overcome these handicaps, communicate with the world, and spread her lectures promoting optimism. An inspiring read for everyone...　　Biographies/Inspirational Pages 84

Sara Crewe *by Frances Burnett*　　　　　　　　　　　　　　ISBN: *1-59462-360-0*　**$9.45**

In the first place, Miss Minchin lived in London. Her home was a large, dull, tall one, in a large, dull square, where all the houses were alike, and all the sparrows were alike, and where all the door-knockers made the same heavy sound...　　Childrens/Classic Pages 88

The Autobiography of Benjamin Franklin *by Benjamin Franklin*　　ISBN: *1-59462-135-7*　**$24.95**

The Autobiography of Benjamin Franklin has probably been more extensively read than any other American historical work, and no other book of its kind has had such ups and downs of fortune. Franklin lived for many years in England, where he was agent...　　Biographies/History Pages 332

Name	
Email	
Telephone	
Address	
City, State ZIP	

☐ Credit Card　　　　　　☐ Check / Money Order

Credit Card Number	
Expiration Date	
Signature	

Please Mail to:　Book Jungle
　　　　　　　　PO Box 2226
　　　　　　　　Champaign, IL 61825
or Fax to:　　　630-214-0564

ORDERING INFORMATION

web: *www.bookjungle.com*
email: *sales@bookjungle.com*
fax: *630-214-0564*
mail: *Book Jungle PO Box 2226 Champaign, IL 61825*
or PayPal *to sales@bookjungle.com*

Please contact us for bulk discounts

DIRECT-ORDER TERMS

**20% Discount if You Order
Two or More Books**
Free Domestic Shipping!
Accepted: Master Card, Visa,
Discover, American Express